AC...   ...CE

ON
POINTE

written by   cover illustration by Claire Almon
...garet Gurevich   interior illustrations by Addy Rivera Sonda

raintree
a Capstone company—publishers for children
www.raintree.co.uk

Raintree is an imprint of Capstone Global Library Limited, a company
incorporated in England and Wales having its registered office at 264 Banbury
Road, Oxford, OX2 7DY – Registered company number: 6695582

www.raintree.co.uk
myorders@raintree.co.uk

Designed by Kayla Rossow
Original illustrations © Capstone Global Library Limited 2019
Originated by Capstone Global Library Ltd
Printed and bound in India

ISBN 978 1 4747 6863 4
23 22 21 20 19
10 9 8 7 6 5 4 3 2 1

British Library Cataloguing in Publication Data
A full catalogue record for this book is available from the British Library.

CONTENTS

CHAPTER 1

READY FOR MORE

I rise on the balls of my feet for the *relevé*, curve my arms in front so my fingertips touch and twirl across the smooth wooden floor. Each time my toes glide across the studio floors at Ms Marianne's Academy of Dance it feels like magic.

Ms Marianne herself paces the floor and monitors our footing, balance and form. Her salt-and-pepper hair is pulled back into its usual bun, and her burgundy scarf matches her leotard.

I bend my knees for a *plié* and smile as the rest of the girls do the same. It's hard to believe I was once nervous about coming here.

My family and I moved from Philadelphia to New Jersey less than a year ago. I didn't want to leave the noises of the city, my friends, my old dance team or my old dance school.

At first I thought I would never fit in. But then I found Ms Marianne's. After a rocky start, I met amazing girls on the dance team who became my best friends. Now Ms Marianne's feels like a second home.

I rise on my tiptoes again and perform a *soutenu* turn, keeping my arms curved in front of me.

"Beautiful form, Jada!" Ms Marianne calls.

I smile in response, keeping my focus on my dancing. Grace Jenkins, one of my best friends, grins and silently claps her hands. Grace is a tap dancer, but everyone at Ms Marianne's is required to take Wednesday's all-team ballet class.

"*Chassé*, ladies!" Ms Marianne says above the music.

I line up beside my two other best friends, Gabby Sanchez and Brie Benson. Even though ballet is supposed to be serious, it's hard to keep a straight face when the four of us get together. Ms Marianne gives us a warning look, but I can tell she's trying to stop herself smiling.

As the music speeds up, my feet glide across the floor, faster and faster.

"*Piqué* turns!" calls Ms Marianne.

Piqué turns are a beginner move, and I've been doing ballet for years, so it's easy to want to breeze through them. But I've learned to be patient and take my time. I keep my arms open wide in second position and move my right foot forward, careful to keep it straight and pointed. My left toe meets my right knee as I turn and close my arms in front of me.

"And one and two and three," Ms Marianne calls as all the dancers do three *piqué* turns in a row. I spot the corner beside the window each time I turn to keep my balance.

We end the class with one of my favourite jumps, the *changement*. I place my feet in fifth position with my right leg in front, toes touching the heels. Then I jump up and land in fifth position, this time with my left leg in front.

When the class finishes, I notice Ms Marianne studying me. I want to find out why, but before I can approach, another dancer starts talking to her. I decide whatever it is can wait. There's somewhere I want to be.

"Come on!" I say to Gabby, Brie and Grace. "Let's go before we miss it."

I lead the way, and in seconds we're standing outside the pointe dance class. We push our faces close to the glass and watch the ballerinas.

My friends all focus on different forms of dance – tap, jazz and hip-hop. But that doesn't stop them from appreciating how challenging pointe is.

Brie lets out a low whistle. "I don't think I could ever trade in my hip-hop trainers for those shoes."

"So true," says Gabby, brushing her dark hair from her eyes. "There are a lot of ballet moves in jazz, but I can't even imagine standing on my toes like that!"

Grace's curly blonde hair sneaks out of its bun as she nods. "Jada can do it." She winks and puts her arm around me.

The ballerinas' strong calf muscles stand out as they *plié*. I run my hand along my own calves. I know they're strong.

"Do you really think so?" I ask my friends hopefully.

"Absolutely!" says Gabby, bumping me with her hip. "I noticed Ms Marianne paying extra attention to your movements today. I bet that's why."

"Yes!" Brie says a little too loudly and blushes. "You should totally talk to her! You'd be amazing at pointe!"

I look at the pointe dancers one more time. Then I close my eyes and picture myself beside them, pointe shoes on, moving gracefully across the floor. Maybe my friends are right. Maybe I'm ready for more.

CHAPTER 2

POINTE POTENTIAL

During ballet practice the next day, I can barely focus. All I can think about is talking to Ms Marianne about pointe. I spent the past twenty-four hours practising the speech in my head, and I'm ready. As soon as the class ends, I rush across the floor and skid to a stop beside Ms Marianne.

"Jada!" Ms Marianne takes a step back to avoid bumping into me.

"S-sorry," I stutter. I clear my throat and try to remember the speech I'd planned.

"What can I do for you?" my teacher asks kindly.

Just spit it out, I tell myself. "I want to take pointe," I say.

Ms Marianne raises an eyebrow and places her index finger on her chin. But she doesn't say anything.

Nervously I continue. "My calves and ankles are strong. I think I'm ready." I remember what my friends told me yesterday and hope I sound confident. "I know I'm ready."

Ms Marianne laces her fingers together and nods. "I think you're ready too. I've been studying you for the past few weeks in class. Your posture and balance have been impressive. You've always been a great dancer, but you've grown even stronger."

I bite my tongue so I don't squeal out loud. If Ms Marianne were Gabby, Brie or Grace, I would grab her hands and jump up and down, but Ms Marianne is too calm for that.

"Thank you!" I exclaim. "I'm so glad to hear you say that. So what's next?"

Ms Marianne laughs. "Pointe is very exciting, but it is a process. First we need to find the right shoes. After that you need to break them in. And after *that* . . ."

After that I zone out. I see Ms Marianne's lips moving, but I can't focus on her words. All I can think about is starting pointe! Besides, I've been dancing for more than seven years. I know I can handle whatever is thrown at me.

"Jada?" Ms Marianne says, bringing me back to planet Earth. She looks worried, but I'm not sure why.

"I can do this," I reassure her. "I can do it."

Ms Marianne nods slowly. "I'm glad you're confident. I just want you to remember that it takes *time* to feel comfortable in the shoes. They *will* hurt."

"I can handle it," I say confidently.

"Just remember that pointe affects some dancers' feet more than others. Even dancers like you, who appear physically ready, may not be mentally ready for the toll the shoes can take."

I don't understand how someone can *seem* ready but not be. Ms Marianne said I was strong and had good balance.

What more do you need? I think. Still, I nod to show I'm listening.

"You are a wonderful dancer," she goes on, "but if – at any time – you decide pointe isn't for you, please speak up. It's not for everyone, and that's *fine*."

This must be the speech she gives to everyone. I want to roll my eyes, but I know that would be rude. "I never step away from a challenge," I say, grinning at her.

Ms Marianne looks as if she wants to say

something else but changes her mind. "Very well," she says. "I'll call your mother, and we'll arrange a time for the three of us to go shopping for pointe shoes. Remember to wear tights."

"Thank you!" I gush. When a sentence has my two favourite words – *pointe* and *shopping* – what could be better?

CHAPTER 3

SHOE SHOPPING

"Come on!" I call over my shoulder to Mum as I run down the street on Saturday.

"I'm trying, but some of us aren't speedy teenagers!" Mum calls as she jogs to match my pace.

Normally when my mum and I go shopping for ballet stuff, I stand in front of the window first and look at the display. But today there's no time to wait.

I head into the shop immediately. Inside, the shelves are full of everything from leotards to shoes to bags with ballerinas embroidered on them.

I look past all the equipment, my eyes scanning the shop for Ms Marianne. She waves to me from the pointe section, and I sprint to join her.

"She's very excited," my mum says as she joins us. She puts her arm around me.

Ms Marianne smiles warmly. "It's a very big deal. I still remember when I got *my* first pair of pointe shoes. I was thirteen, just like Jada."

Let's just start! I want to shout.

A short, older woman walks up to us. "I'm Doreen, and I'll be your fitter today," she says.

"Fitter?" I ask, confused. "When I bought ballet shoes, I just tried on my shoe size."

"Not with pointe shoes, my dear," says Doreen. "We need to measure the width of your foot, arch height and length of your toe. The shape of your foot also matters. Have a seat, please."

Doreen motions to the seat as if she's inviting a queen to sit on a throne, and I giggle. Once I'm seated she moves my feet back and forth. Then she asks me to stand and sit so she can see my feet at different angles. She scribbles notes onto a small, yellow pad.

When she's finished – more than twenty minutes later – Doreen disappears behind a curtain at the back of the shop to look for shoes that best match my feet. Soon she's back with a trolley piled high with boxes. All the top pointe shoe brands are there.

"I can't believe these are all for me!" I exclaim as I grab one of the boxes and throw the lid off.

"Put these on your toes first," says Doreen handing me something soft that looks like toe mittens. "They'll make dancing in your pointe shoes less painful."

I put the mittens on. Then I shove my foot into the shoe and . . . stop. Something's wrong.

"They're all going to be uncomfortable at first," Ms Marianne says, reading my face.

"That's why I have a list of what to look for," says Doreen, flipping a page on her notepad.

My shoulders slump a little. Apparently when Ms Marianne said, "It is a process," she didn't just mean dancing.

"As your feet are a little wide," says Doreen, "I chose shoes with a square box." She points to the top of the shoe. "I also think a shorter vamp – the length of the box – is best so that you can get fully up on pointe. There's also the shank, the part that supports the arch. Your teacher and I like a softer shank so the shoes can be broken in more easily. It will help strengthen your arches, which is very important so you don't hurt yourself."

I nod slowly. Getting pointe shoes is not going to be simple.

"Can you wiggle your toes?" Ms Marianne asks.

"Yes!" I say happily.

"Then they're the wrong fit," says Doreen. "They should fit like a glove. No wiggle room."

"Oh." I take off the shoes and try on another pair. "Definitely no wiggle room here. My toes are on top of each other."

"Off," says Doreen. "Your toes shouldn't be squished together either."

I sigh and try on another pair. And another. And another. More than an hour later, I *finally* have my shoes.

"Thanks so much," my mum says to Doreen. "This was quite an experience!"

"Now I can go home and dance!" I say, my excitement returning.

Doreen and Ms Marianne exchange looks.

"What?" I say. I can hear the whine in my voice.

"You need to sew on the ribbons first, then learn how to tie them. Even then, I don't want you trying any ballet moves without me," says Ms Marianne firmly. "I mentioned that when we talked the other day."

I feel my face get hot. That must have been the part I wasn't really listening to.

I put the shoes back into their box and lace up my trainers. Ms Marianne and Doreen tell my mum how to sew the ribbons onto my shoes. Then they tell us how to lace the shoes. I try to pay attention, but it's hard. All I can think is that it will be *forever* before I actually get to dance in my new pointe shoes.

"Congratulations!" Ms Marianne says as we leave the shop. "Why don't you come to the studio tomorrow morning? We'll start breaking them in."

"Tomorrow? Really?" I say, feeling relieved. "I'll be there!"

Maybe forever isn't as far away as I thought.

CHAPTER 4

POINTE READY

"I'm pointe ready!" I say as I run into the studio the next morning.

Ms Marianne laughs. "I'm still waiting for my coffee to kick in."

"I'm so hyped up, I don't need caffeine." I take my pointe shoes out of the box and slip them on. My mum sewed the ribbons on last night, and I proudly tie the ribbons in a bow.

"Very nice," Ms Marianne says. "I just have a few minor adjustments. First of all, never tie the ribbons in a bow. Bows can come undone. You should double knot them, just between your ankle bone and your Achilles tendon."

"Oh, OK," I say, nodding.

"Then you tuck in the knot and the loose ends of the ribbons," she continues. "We don't want to see the knot. Here, I'll show you."

Ms Marianne laces the ribbons around my ankle. I watch carefully. Then she undoes her work and hands the ribbons to me so I can practise tying them. It takes four tries to get them perfect.

"See how the ribbons cross in the middle of your ankle?" Ms Marianne points out. I nod. "That's how you know you've tied them correctly," she explains. "Ribbons help support your ankles, so we can't cut corners and risk injury."

Just like when we were shopping for shoes, I'm eager to get started. But one look at Ms Marianne's serious face tells me all these little details are just as important as dancing.

"I understand," I say.

"Good," says Ms Marianne. "I need you to be patient. Because as I said the other day, it's—"

I grin. "A process."

"That's right." Ms Marianne winks at me. "Before you walk on the shoes, we need to crush the box. Softening the front of the shoe will make it fit better around your toe joints."

"Oh!" I say excitedly. "I saw that on YouTube. Dancers slam the front of the shoe inside a door."

Ms Marianne looks horrified. "We are *not* doing that," she says firmly. "Too many things could go wrong, like crushing your finger. Step on it with your heel instead."

The door idea seemed fun, but I do as Ms Marianne says. I untie the ribbons, slip my shoes off and place them on the ground. Then I use my heels to soften each shoe's toe box.

"There you go," says Ms Marianne. "Now hold the canvas of each shoe with both hands and pull it up so it bends. It's called bending the shank. It will help with the fit. Be careful not to snap the shank in half."

I follow Ms Marianne's instructions, treating my shoes like glass. They're so special, I don't want to ruin them. When I'm finished, I look at her. I know these steps are important, but I'm ready to dance!

Ms Marianne's eyes twinkle. "Do you think you're ready to begin now?"

"Yes!" I exclaim.

"Fabulous," says Ms Marianne. "To start breaking them in, I want you to walk across the floor and back in *demi pointe*. That's just walking on the balls of your feet, not on your toes."

"Got it," I say. It may be only *demi pointe*, but at least I'll get to do something in my new shoes!

I put my shoes back on and tie the ribbons, just like Ms Marianne showed me. Then I rise onto the balls of my feet and take my first steps.

Almost immediately I feel a pull on my calves. There's a tightening in my toes too. I keep going until I reach the mirror. Then I turn around and walk back to Ms Marianne.

"How do the shoes feel?" she asks.

I shrug and keep walking. The truth is they hurt, but I don't want to admit that. Not when I'm finally getting to use them.

"You looked good out there," says Ms Marianne. "Can you try that one more time?"

I want to say I'd like a break, but we've barely done anything. A serious dancer would push through, wouldn't she?

"Of course," I say. I rise onto the balls of my feet again and start walking.

"Let's do a few *relevés* and grand *pliés* at the barre," chirps Ms Marianne.

"Sounds good," I say brightly, trying to match Ms Marianne's cheery tone.

I must not sound entirely convincing, because Ms Marianne studies my face. "Jada, it's normal for your feet to be uncomfortable. If you aren't ready for more today, it's *completely* fine. You're a beginner."

I bristle. I haven't thought of myself as a *beginner* since I was five years old. I take a deep breath and let it out.

"Thank you," I say, putting a fake smile on my face, "but I can do it."

I place my hand on the barre, bend my knees, and lift my heels as I come up for the *grand plié*.

"Again," says Ms Marianne. "To dance *en pointe*, it's very important you get used to the motions and break in the shoes."

I nod. I finish the *grand pliés* and practise rising to high *demi pointe* for the *relevés*.

"Up," says Ms Marianne, "and down. And up. And down."

I sigh. Not only are the shoes uncomfortable, but the moves are boring. I feel as if I'm five all over again.

Finally Ms Marianne claps. "OK, I think that's enough for today. You're off to a great start! Practise these moves at home, and I'll see you at the beginner pointe class on Tuesday."

"Then I'll finally be able to stand on my toes?" I ask.

Ms Marianne nods. "Yes. I know it's hard, but be patient. It may have been hundreds of years ago," she teases, "but I remember how you feel."

This time when I smile, it's real. "Thank you." I don't know if Ms Marianne really knows how I feel, but it's still nice of her to say it.

CHAPTER 5

BEGINNER BLUES

Can't wait to hear about your first pointe class!!!

I grin when the message from Brie pops up on the group text I have with her, Grace and Gabby on Monday afternoon. My friends' support always gives me confidence.

Today's class will be great! I tell myself. Sunday was about breaking in my shoes, but today I'll actually get to go on my toes.

I'm already in the studio, waiting for the class to start. Everyone around me is lacing up their ribbons. I do the same, then grab an open space at the barre to practise my *pliés* and *demi pointes*.

Finally I rise to my toes. I feel the difference immediately and go back down. I stretch my ankles and try again. My ankles and toes hurt, but I shake it off.

It's a process, I tell myself, echoing Ms Marianne.

A moment later, Ms Marianne herself walks in. She claps her hands to signal the start of the class. "Places, ladies! We will begin with the *sous-sus*."

That's such a beginner move! I think. *I can do this!*

I place my feet in fifth position, my toes and heels touching, and sink down into a *plié*. Then I spring back up onto the tips of my toes.

"Ouch," I mutter as I stumble.

I do the same move again – slower this time – and get it. Sort of. I watch the other dancers match Ms Marianne's rhythm.

Every other girl makes the rise from *plié* to *sous-sus* look easy. A *sous-sus* is a move I've done countless times. It *should* be easy.

You've never done it in pointe shoes! a voice in my head taunts.

"*Plié, sous-sus.* Again!" calls Ms Marianne as she walks around.

I sink down and try to spring back up, but I stumble. No one else does. No one else looks like she's in pain. I do the moves again and wince.

"Two feet!" Ms Marianne calls.

We *plié* and quickly rise to our toes while holding onto the barre.

"Two feet! One foot! Two feet! One foot!" Ms Marianne sings as she walks around the room.

I grit my teeth as I *plié* and rise to two toes, then one, two, then one. My calves and ankles are killing me. I feel my toes scrape painfully against the insides of my pointe shoes.

Is the skin scraping off? Are they bruised and bloody? Is it supposed to be this painful? I try not to think about it.

"How are you, Jada?" Ms Marianne asks as she walks behind me.

I force a smile, but don't say anything. I don't want her to think I can't handle it.

Ms Marianne pats my shoulder. "You're doing a great job, but to be on the safe side, why don't you change into your ballet shoes after the next exercise? I don't want you to overdo it on the first day."

I want to protest – I should be able to keep up with the other dancers. I'm not some beginner. But before I can say anything, Ms Marianne is already moving away.

"Let's step away from the barre now," Ms Marianne instructs. "Keep moving through your warm-ups."

I gingerly let go of the barre. Doing these exercises with the barre for support was hard enough. Without the barre it will be torture.

Don't think about the pain. You can do it. I keep repeating the phrases in my head as I *plié*, then spring to my toes, but they're not helping.

Suddenly Ms Marianne is beside me again. "I think it's best to stop now," she says quietly.

No matter how much I fake it, I can't trick her. I walk to the side, take off my shoes and slip on my ballet slippers. Even though my toes, ankles and calves are sore, my ballet slippers feel like clouds.

I watch the rest of the dancers finish their warm-up, then twirl on their toes. They look so amazing.

My heart sinks. *Were they ever in my very painful shoes?* I wonder. *Will I ever look like them?*

CHAPTER 6

A BiG ADJUSTMENT

"What happened?" Grace asks the next day, staring at my bandaged feet. We're all gathered in the studio to warm up before our all-team ballet class.

When I took off my tights after pointe class last night, my toes were bleeding. Blisters were forming on my heels and the sides of my feet. This morning, my feet were still a mess.

I adjust the bandages and carefully pull my tights on over the top. "Pointe class happened," I reply.

Brie frowns. "Sorry," she says. "That looks painful."

I shrug as if it doesn't bother me. Except it does. "I looked it up online, and all the ballet sites say it's common to get blisters when you first start pointe," I say.

"Maybe you should talk to Ms Marianne," Gabby suggests.

I shake my head. "I don't want her to say I can't do it."

Brie bites her lip. "Are you sure?"

I slip on my ballet slippers and *plié*, trying not to grimace. "See? No problem."

My friends exchange worried looks, but before they can say anything else, Ms Marianne enters the studio. Everyone moves to the barre for warm-ups.

Plié and up. *Plié* and up. I straighten my back to keep smooth lines in my torso.

"Lovely form, ladies," says Ms Marianne. "Now *relevé*!"

I rise to my tiptoes, and my ankles hurt. I bite my lip to stop myself from crying out as I slowly lower my feet to the floor.

"*Relevé, arabesque*," Ms Marianne calls as she walks across the floor.

And up, I tell myself as I rise to the balls of my feet again. I lift my leg behind me for the *arabesque* and try to block out the pain in my ankles.

Each time Ms Marianne looks in my direction, I work on keeping my face emotionless. If she sees I'm in pain, she'll think I can't handle pointe.

"Line up for grand *jetés*," Ms Marianne instructs.

My stomach drops. If I'm feeling pain with simple moves like *pliés* and *relevés*, the jumps will be agony.

You can do this, I tell myself. If only pep talks were enough.

When it's my turn to leap across the floor,
I close my eyes and hope for the best. My feet
leave the ground, and I do the splits in the air.

Thud.

All too soon, I land on the hard, wooden
floor. This time I can't help crying out.

Ms Marianne comes up behind me. "I think
you should sit out the rest of the class," she says.
"Your feet need to recover."

Tears spring to my eyes. I can't keep up in
pointe, and now I'm being forced to sit out
ballet too?

"I'm fine," I insist. "I can shake it off."

Ms Marianne puts her hand on my arm.
"Jada, your safety is the most important thing,"
she says firmly. "Have a seat."

I grit my teeth to stop myself crying in front
of everyone. Then I grab my water bottle and
walk out of the class.

Through the large window beside the door
I watch everyone else *jeté, pirouette* and *chassé*
across the floor. My friends smile in between
jumps, twirls and glides.

I wanted a challenge, but this is not what
I'd imagined. I expected pointe to be hard, but I
never thought my ballet would suffer too.

CHAPTER 7

A LOT LIKE GIVING UP

I read online that calluses form on your toes the longer you do pointe, so instead of resting my feet that night, I decide to practise the moves from my first pointe class. It's painful, but I know I'm ready for pointe. I must be.

The next morning, I realize that pushing through the pain might have been a *bad* decision. My feet are in even worse shape than yesterday.

I change the bloody plasters and wrap bandages around my sore ankles. Each time that my heels graze the back of my trainers, I feel the blisters scrape. But I'm determined not to let that stop me.

My soft ballet slippers will feel better, I tell myself as I head to the studio for my ballet class. I get there half an hour early. Ms Marianne is already there.

"How are you feeling today?" she asks when I walk in.

"Getting there," I say with a brave smile.

Ms Marianne looks concerned. "Jada, I'd like to talk to you for a minute," she says. "Remember when I said you reminded me of myself?"

I nod. "I won't disappoint you."

"That's not what I meant," she says gently. "You're a wonderful dancer, and I know how eager you were to start pointe. I was eager too. My ankles were strong, and I was great at my jumps. I was sure I was ready."

I can see where this conversation is going. I frown. "I *am* ready."

Ms Marianne smiles sympathetically. "I let you try pointe because your ankles *are* strong. But even the best dancers progress at different stages. Starting earlier or later doesn't make someone better. I started at your age, but it turned out I wasn't ready. It was painful, and I *hated* that it stopped me from dancing in my normal ballet classes."

I'm surprised. "What did you do?"

"I took a break until I was more prepared. When I started pointe again at sixteen, my ankles and feet were stronger. I was mentally ready, and I knew what to expect. It was much easier." She looks at me and raises one eyebrow.

I look down at the floor. I know Ms Marianne wants me to make the same decision she did. A part of me wants that too. But another part of me feels as if stopping now is the same thing as giving up.

"Think about it," says Ms Marianne.

I raise my head to look at Ms Marianne's kind eyes. "I will."

"There's something else," she continues. "I noticed you limping before–"

I cut her off. "I'm fine now."

"Jada," Ms Marianne says firmly, "it's my responsibility to make sure my students are safe. Before the class starts, I'd like you to show me some basic moves and jumps. If you can do them, I'll back off. If not, I'm afraid you'll have to sit out today's class."

"What would you like me to do?" I ask quietly, walking to the barre by the mirrors.

"Let's start with *plié* to *relevé*," says Ms Marianne.

I bend my knees as I lower myself towards the floor. Then I slowly straighten my legs as I rise to the balls of my feet.

The whole time I wonder if my teacher is as frustrated with me as I am with myself.

After a moment, Ms Marianne turns on the music. I try to keep up with it, but my ankles throb, making it impossible.

Ms Marianne frowns. "That's all I need to see. I'm not going to torture you with *chassés* and *jetés*."

"Do you want me to stay and watch the others?" I ask. That's what I had to do when I sprained my ankle last year. Ms Marianne thinks it's important for dancers to support their teammates and keep the routine fresh in their minds, even if they can't dance.

Ms Marianne studies my face and shakes her head. "Not if you don't want to. But promise me two things. One, stay off the pointe shoes. You can't heal if you keep pushing yourself."

I hang my head.

"Two, think about what I said before. It's not giving up. Just . . . waiting."

I feel a tear slipping down my cheek. It sounds a lot like giving up to *me*. Still, I mumble what Ms Marianne wants to hear. "I promise."

CHAPTER 8

DECISION TIME

"You have another pointe class tomorrow, right?" asks Grace on Saturday night. She, Gabby, Brie and I are all sitting in Gabby's basement snacking on the crispy plantains her *abuela* made. We're all spending the night here tonight.

"That's the plan," I say, crunching down on a plantain.

"Are your feet better?" Brie asks, reaching across me for another plantain.

"Finally," I say.

"But?" Grace says. She always seems to be able to read my mind.

I haven't told my friends about my conversation with Ms Marianne. I've been a bit afraid they'll agree with her. Or maybe I've been afraid they *won't*. I wring my hands.

"Ms Marianne and I talked on Thursday. . . ." I say. "She thinks I should stop pointe. For now, at least."

"Did she say why?" Gabby asks. "Because your feet have been hurting?"

"That's a big part of it," I say. "But she also thinks it's taking me away from ballet, and I'm struggling to do both."

"What do *you* think?" asks Grace.

I'm so confused I don't know where to start. "I really want to do pointe. I was so sure I was ready for it," I say, trying to weed through all the thoughts in my head.

Brie furrows her brow. "And now you think you're not?"

I throw my hands up, frustrated. "I don't know! I don't know what to think. My feet were bleeding for days. My ankles hurt so much, I could barely do a basic *plié*." I wince, remembering the pain.

"Wow," says Gabby. "I knew your feet were bothering you, but I didn't realize they were that bad!"

I blush. "I didn't want anyone to think I couldn't handle pointe." I pause. "I was trying to convince *myself* I was fine."

Gabby chews the inside of her cheek, deep in thought. "Did Ms Marianne have any advice?"

I sigh. "Just that I should take a break and try again when I'm older."

Brie looks thoughtful. "This isn't exactly the same, but remember when Gabby and I both went after the solo last year?"

"Unfortunately," I say, wrinkling my nose. The whole experience almost ruined their friendship.

Brie makes a face too and laughs. "Yeah, not an experience I want to repeat. But the *good* part about it was that the solo went to a more experienced dancer. It taught us that if we keep practising, we'll get there one day too."

"Right," adds Gabby. "There's more to learn. We don't have to do it all right now."

"And Ms Marianne is always adding new classes," Grace adds. "You never know what might pop up."

I get up and pace around Gabby's basement. My friends make good points, but I know what's really bothering me. "But isn't it like failing?" I ask softly.

"No way," says Grace. "Our best friend is not a failure. Think of all you've accomplished."

"New state, new dance team, new friends," Gabby says, counting on her fingers.

"Even last year when you hurt your ankle–" Brie starts.

"Oh, you mean when I felt sorry for myself?" I interrupt.

Brie waves her hand. "Maybe a bit, but then you pushed yourself to practise and get better. You did amazingly well at our first competition."

Grace jumps off the sofa and puts her arm around me. "You know you'll go back to pointe." She pauses. "Right?"

I think about what my friends are saying. Then I consider what will happen if I stay with pointe now. Chances are it won't be any different from last week. My ankles will throb. My toes will bleed. It'll be back to bandages and plasters. The thought of hobbling around, not being able to even do ballet, is unbearable.

Grace nudges me. "Jada?"

A part of me still hates the idea of stopping something I've started, but Grace is right. I can use this time to keep getting better at ballet. Keep doing what I love. And when I'm ready, follow my pointe dream too.

"Of course I'll go back to it," I say.

"Then that's your answer," says Gabby.

CHAPTER 9

NOT GIVING UP

The next morning, my stomach is a jumble of nerves. I know Ms Marianne will agree with my decision, but I'm still nervous about telling her.

"Jada!" Ms Marianne says when I walk into the studio the next morning. "You're here early."

I make my way over and take a deep breath. I don't know why getting the words out is so hard. "I thought about what you said the other day," I start. "You were right. I'll try pointe again when I'm a bit older."

I know I'm making the right decision. I also know Ms Marianne thinks this is the right decision, and *she's* the expert.

It was the idea of giving up that was holding me back, I realized. There was a knot in my stomach, scaring me into thinking that this was my one chance to advance. But after talking to my friends and really thinking it through, I realized I would never let myself give up on my dreams.

"Oh, honey," Ms Marianne says, giving me a hug. "I know it's hard, but it's very important you don't see this as a forever decision. It's just–"

"Waiting," I say quietly.

"That's right. You're a talented dancer, and I don't want you to miss out on doing what you love. It's OK to wait until you're ready. And" – she pauses – "this is not giving up."

I nod. It's still hard not to feel sad. I don't want to run away from things. I only want to run *towards* something.

"I want to hear you say it," Ms Marianne says. "Come on, humour me. 'This is not giving up.'"

"This is not giving up," I repeat, feeling silly.

"Again," says Ms Marianne.

"This is not giving up," I say.

Even though I finally believe these words, hearing them out loud makes me feel even better about my decision. I smile. "Thank you."

"I should be thanking *you*," Ms Marianne replies. "You inspired me to start a new class."

My eyes widen. "*I* did?"

"You brought back all the feelings I had when I had to stop pointe. It made me think that maybe there's a better way," says Ms Marianne. "Beginning next week, I'm starting a weekly pre-pointe class. We'll strengthen your ankles and learn new dancing techniques. The goal will be to get dancers' feet pointe ready *before* they start wearing pointe shoes."

"That sounds amazing!" I exclaim. It's just like Grace said: *You never know what might pop up!*

"I know you want a challenge and a chance to learn something new," continues Ms Marianne. "This is a way to do that, minus the pain and stress. When you're ready to try pointe again, you'll be that much closer to success."

My stomach is jumpy again, but this time it's from excitement. I walked into Ms Marianne's a bundle of nerves, but I'm leaving filled with new possibilities.

ABOUT THE AUTHOR

Margaret Gurevich is the author of many books for kids, including *Gina's Balance*, *Aerials and Envy* and the award-winning Chloe by Design series. She has also written for *National Geographic Kids* and Penguin Young Readers. While Margaret hasn't done performance dance since she was a tween, this series has inspired her to take dance classes again. She lives in New York, USA, with her son and husband.

ABOUT THE ILLUSTRATOR

Addy Rivera Sonda is a Mexican illustrator currently living in California, USA. She loves colour and nature. They inspire her to think that stories and art are slowly but surely changing the way people understand themselves and perceive others, building empathy and a more inclusive world.

GLOSSARY

abuela grandmother

accomplish do something successfully

Achilles tendon body part that connects the muscles of the lower leg to the heel's bone

barre horizontal wooden bar used by dancers for support and balance

bristle show signs of anger

plantain greenish fruit of a type of banana plant that is eaten cooked and is larger, less sweet and more starchy than an ordinary banana

posture position of your body

rhythm regular, repeated pattern of beats, sounds, activity or movements

unbearable something so bad or unpleasant that you cannot stand it

TALK ABOUT IT!

1. Jada is excited about starting to learn pointe, but Ms Marianne tells her she might not be ready. Talk about a time you felt ready to learn something at school or in a club, but were told you weren't ready.

2. When Jada begins practising pointe, she doesn't tell Ms Marianne or her friends how much pain she's in. Talk about why you think she stays quiet.

3. Jada is worried people will think she's a failure if she waits to continue learning pointe. Why do you think she feels this way?

WRITE ABOUT IT!

1. Jada and her friends each belong to a different dance group, practising ballet, tap dance, jazz and hip-hop. Write about which dance group you would join if you went to Ms Marianne's Academy of Dance.

2. Starting pointe lessons gives Jada some problems. Write down some of the dangers of starting pointe.

3. Jada begins pointe before she's really ready for it. Write down some reasons she'll be more prepared to start pointe the next time she tries.

MORE ABOUT POINTE

When you think about ballet, what do you picture? Graceful ballerinas balanced on the tips of their toes? If that's the case, you're actually thinking about pointe. Pointe is a technique – and part of ballet – in which a dancer supports all of her body weight on the tips of her toes while wearing special shoes called pointe shoes.

So what does it take to be pointe ready? There are several factors to think about, including a dancer's strength, age, technique and experience:

- Typically a dancer should have at least 2–4 years of ballet experience before attempting pointe work.

- Most dancers don't start learning pointe until 12–14 years of age. Before that, the bones of the foot aren't fully developed. Permanent foot injuries could occur as a result of starting pointe too early.

- In addition to strong feet, pointe dancers must have strong ankles and legs. These are crucial for a dancer to be able to stay on pointe for the length of a routine. A strong core helps with balance and is essential to ensure a dancer doesn't roll her feet while dancing.

- During the first year of pointe, dancers can expect to take 3–4 ballet classes per week.

DANCE MOVES EXPLAINED

Want to learn more? Here are a few moves all ballet dancers should know:

arabesque ballet move where the dancer stands on one leg and extends the other behind

chassé ballet move where the dancer makes quick, gliding steps

jeté move in ballet where the dancer extends one leg, then jumps with the other

pirouette full turn on the front of one foot

plié move where a dancer stands with his or her feet turned out, then bends and straightens the knees

relevé ballet move where a dancer looks as if he or she is standing on his or her toes

sous-sus ballet move that means "over-under" and describes when a dancer quickly rises from *demi-plié* onto pointe, placing the back foot closely behind the front in fifth position with fully stretched legs

soutenu turn in ballet where the dancer turns in *sous-sus* or fifth position *en pointe* and ends with the opposite foot in front

THE FUN DOESN'T STOP HERE!

DISCOVER MORE AT
WWW.RAINTREE.CO.UK